our
generation®

This is Lorelei's story.

L O R E L E I ™

THE INCREDIBLE ICE CREAM PROJECT

BY

SUSAN HUGHES

ILLUSTRATED BY GÉRALDINE CHARETTE

An Our Generation® *book*

MAISON JOSEPH BATTAT LTD. *Publisher*

Our Generation® Books is a registered trademark of Maison Joseph Battat Ltd.
Text copyright © 2016 by Susan Hughes
Characters portrayed in this book are fictitious. Any references to historical
events, real people, or real locales are used fictitiously. Other names,
characters, places, and incidents are products of the author's imagination,
and any resemblance to actual events or locales or persons, living or dead,
is entirely coincidental.
All rights reserved, including the right of reproduction in whole or in part
in any form.
ISBN: 978-0-9843722-5-6
Printed in China

Thank you to the Battat editorial team for their help in creating this book, especially editor Joanne Burke Casey and designer Loredana Ramacieri.

Read all the adventures in the
Our Generation® Book Series

Read more about **Our Generation®** books and dolls online:
www.ogdolls.com

CONTENTS

EXTRA! EXTRA! READ ALL ABOUT IT!
Big words, wacky words, powerful words, funny words...
what do they all mean? They are marked with this symbol *.
Look them up in the Glossary at the end of this book.

Chapter One

DAIRY FARM TROUBLE

I paused on the steps of the school bus. "See you tomorrow, Abril," I called over my shoulder. "Oh, and don't forget to ask your parents if you can come over after school tomorrow. Corinne and Carter are coming, too."

Abril is my best friend, and she lives on the farm next to ours. The school bus picks her up first every morning, just before me. And it drops her off last, after me, at the end of our school day at Sunny Skies Elementary School.

"Okey-dokey, Lorelei!" Abril called from her seat, with a wave.

I thanked Mrs. Fisher, the bus driver, and stepped down from the bus. As it headed off toward Abril's farm, I walked up the long gravel drive to Daisy Dairy, which is our dairy farm. I breathed a sigh of happiness. It was a beautiful day near the end of June, and summer vacation would begin soon. Fields of corn stretched away on either side of me. A red-winged blackbird* sang from the fence post.

I can't imagine living anywhere else on Earth. I am so lucky. The farm has been in our family for many, many years. My great-grandparents first raised dairy cows here. When their daughter was born, they named her Daisy. She became my granny! The farm was named "Daisy Dairy" after her and they passed the farm down to my granny about 40 years ago.

My granny and grandpa raised my dad on the farm. After he finished high school, Dad studied business and agricultural management* in college. Instead of coming back to the farm after graduation, he decided to work as an agricultural consultant* for several large businesses. That's when he met and married Mom.

But when Grandpa died, Dad and Mom decided to come back and help Gran continue to run the farm. Soon after, I was born. My little brother, Joey, came along a couple of years later.

I smiled as I neared our house, admiring the colors of the countryside. I love the light in the morning, when the sun is rising and the world is filled with soft pastel* colors. I love the vivid blue of the sky when the sun is high and bright. I like seeing the sky fill with puffy white clouds or darken with purple and black thunderclouds. I love the orange and red streaks of the sunset.

The fields change colors through the seasons: green in the spring, golden in the late summer, white with snow in the winter. I'm always getting out my pencils, pastels* and paints and trying to put what I see around me onto paper.

"Hey Lorelei, Gran and I made oatmeal cookies today!" Joey called from the porch of our old stone farmhouse. "Want one?"

I bounded up the steps and my brother held out a plate, offering me a freshly baked cookie.

"Thanks, little bro." I smiled at him, grabbed a cookie and hurried inside.

"Hello, Gran! Hi, Mom!" I called.

I didn't hear Mom answer, but I knew she was probably in her home office. She does the accounting* for our farm, and also for several other small farmers and some businesses in town.

I ran upstairs to my room, dropped my backpack on my bed, grabbed my sketchbook and pencils, and zoomed back downstairs. Spotting Gran in the kitchen, I made a detour so I could give her a quick hug.

"You're off to the barn," she said, with a nod. "See you at dinnertime."

Everyone in our family knows my routine. Pretty much every single day when I get home from school, I head to the barn to say hello to our dairy cows. I know the name of each one of them!

We have 82 Holstein cows on our farm. Holsteins are famous for producing more milk than any other breed of cow. We take really good care of our cows. Every day, each one eats about 40 pounds of food and drinks as much water as a bathtub would hold!

Dad and our farmhand, Todd, milk the cows twice a day in the milking barn. The rest of the time, when the weather is mild, the cows hang out in the yard beside the barn or graze* in the pasture*.

When it's really hot or really cold, the cows prefer to stay inside the barn. The barn is heated in the winter and air-conditioned in the summer, so the temperature is always nice for them, plus they have room to move around. Gran likes to joke, "Those cows are spoiled! They're better looked after than we are!"

I entered the wide doors of the milking barn. There were dozens of cows, happily chewing their feed.

"Hello Maybelle and Bernadette. Hello Isabelle and Confetti and Clover," I called.

Bessie and Whittaker looked over at me with their big brown eyes.

Holstein cows are black and white. Abril thinks it's funny that I can tell them apart, even though I've explained to her that each cow has a unique* pattern. "Just like a snowflake," she says.

"Mooooo!" they lowed*.

"Moo to you, too," I replied, with a grin. "Do you all want to be my models for today?"

I grabbed a stool, sat down, and opened my sketchbook. Sometimes I paint pictures of the cows, but mostly I like to create cartoons or comic strips about them. I even have the cows saying things to one another.

I do caricatures, too. That's a type of drawing. It exaggerates* one or more features of the person or thing being drawn. That way, I can really show each cow's personality. For example, today I saw how Whittaker was using her tail to swish away the flies, so when I drew her tail, I turned the end of it into a flyswatter!

Maybe I'll show this one to Abril, I decided. *I can always count on her to say something nice about my cartoons and caricatures.* I would never show them to anyone else, though. What if they didn't think they were funny? Just the thought

15

of anyone criticizing* my work makes me feel uncomfortable. I'm such a coward!

I turned the page and sketched Bessie. I was just starting work on a caricature of Clover when I heard Dad's voice.

It must be almost milking time, I thought. Dad and Todd milk the cows in the morning around dawn, and then again in the evening, just before dinner. Sometimes Dad lets me help him in the barn, and even Joey sometimes pitches in. I especially like it when we get to feed the new calves a bottle of milk, or strap on their blankets to keep them warm at night.

But Joey usually teases me when we help out together. It makes me feel embarrassed, even though Joey is very sweet and he's not even trying to be mean. He calls me a "fumblebumbler," and I guess he's right. I have spilled buckets of grain everywhere. And lots of times I've tripped on the barn cats, too. Gran says it's because my thoughts are away exploring life's colors and shapes. Gran is so wonderful. She knows how to turn absolutely anything awkward or bad into something good.

I heard Dad's voice, and then Todd's voice, but not the words they were saying. *I'll poke my head around the wall and say hi to them,* I decided.

When I did, I could suddenly hear Dad quite clearly. "Yes, costs are going up," he was saying in a worried tone. "Costs to feed the cows, vet* costs, costs to heat and cool the barn. Small dairy farms are in trouble."

I froze. *Small dairy farms are in trouble? We have a small dairy farm. Is our farm in trouble?*

I heard Todd's voice. "...sell the cows? Sell the farm?"

Sell the cows? Sell the farm? What? I couldn't hear Dad's answer. I couldn't hear anything. My ears were ringing. My heart was pounding.

It would be horrible to give up the farm— just horrible! Is it possible? Could our own farm really be in trouble?

Chapter Two

LEARNING THE TRUTH

I'm usually hungry at dinnertime, but tonight I poked at my salad. I pushed my noodles from one side of the plate to the other.

Joey had bragged that he'd gathered seven eggs that morning from the chickens. Dad told us that he had gotten the new part for the tractor and it was almost repaired.

I half-listened as Mom told us all about trying to figure out the new accounting computer program she was using.

Then there was silence.

Sell the farm? Sell all our 82 lovely dairy cows? Will I have to leave my Sunny Skies school? Will I ever see Abril again?

Suddenly, I felt Mom's hand on my arm, and I jumped. She stared at me, frowning. "Lorelei, are you alright, honey?"

I couldn't speak. I nodded.

"You haven't said much during dinner," Gran said.

"Are you sure you're OK?" Dad asked.

Again, I nodded *yes*. Then I looked at their four faces, all worried about me, and I shook my head, *no*. It all came out in a rush.

"I was in the barn, sketching. Sketching the cows. I overheard you and Todd, Dad. You were talking about the farm. About how small dairy farms are in trouble. I wasn't trying to eavesdrop*, Dad, really."

Dad smiled reassuringly*.

"Dad, I heard Todd say something about selling our cows. About selling the farm." I swallowed hard. "Dad, are you thinking that we might have to do that? Do we have to sell our farm and move?"

"Move?" Joey said, in a tiny voice. He looked like he might be about to cry. "We have to move?"

19

Dad was shaking his head. "No, Lorelei. No, Joey. It's alright. We don't have to sell the farm."

Gran kissed the top of Joey's head. Mom patted my hand.

"Lorelei, you didn't hear our conversation correctly. So I'm glad you're asking about this," Dad said. He put down his knife and fork. "Todd and I *were* talking about small dairy farms and how many of them are finding it hard to survive. But we weren't talking about us, about our farm."

I took a deep breath. *Phew.*

"We're lucky, because we make enough money to get by just fine. We grow corn for our cows and we sell the extra. Your mom has a good job and earns money for our family. And Gran helps out, raising the chickens and looking after you two rascals." Dad smiled at Joey and me.

"But not everyone is as lucky as we are. And just because *our* family is OK, it doesn't mean that we shouldn't worry about other families running small dairy farms. They are working hard to produce milk, not only to drink, but also to use for making other dairy products, such as cheese, butter and yogurt. Lots of people rely on them. But many farmers are having to sell their farms. They can't keep up with the rising costs. They're being replaced by larger dairy farms that own thousands of cows."

Gran shook her head. "It's sad. Very sad."

Still listening to the conversation, Mom got up to clear the table and I got up to help, too.

"I love knowing that we're providing milk to so many people in this town, Butterton, and in the cities beyond," continued Gran. "But our dairy farm is more than a business to me; it's our way of life. And I know that's how other people with dairy farms must feel as well."

"I agree," said Mom, as she set a plate of oatmeal cookies on the table. "It's a part of our country's heritage*. It's worth saving, I believe."

I was bursting with feelings. Relief that our farm was safe. Concern for our community. Pride that my parents and my grandmother cared so much about others.

"I wish there was something we could do," I said. "I wish we could help!"

"Lorelei, you are very resourceful*," Gran said. "I'm certain that if you put your mind to it, you'll come up with a great idea for how we can help out!"

"I agree!" said Dad, as Mom nodded.

"Me too," said Joey.

"And now, enjoy the cookies that Joey and I made today," Gran suggested. Lifting the jug on the table, she asked, with a twinkle in her eye, "More milk, anyone?"

Chapter Three

SUMMER PLANS

"Our plans for the summer?" asked Corinne, pointing first to herself, and then to her twin brother, Carter.

"Yes," I replied. It was Friday afternoon. My friends and I sat on bales of hay in my family's "old" barn. It was built many years ago and now we use it for storing bedding hay, farming equipment, and other bits and pieces.

"We'll be doing lots and lots of swimming. And you can come over to our place for a swim, too!" Corinne said.

"Mom and Dad are so busy on the farm that they hardly ever have time to take us to the beach in town," said Carter. "So we're having a swimming pool built in this summer."

"Wow!" said Abril. "That sounds great."

I agreed. I like swimming—but not in the lake at Butterton Park. Too many of the town kids swim there. I don't know any of them, and I'm not really good at swimming. I worry that they might laugh at me if I do something dumb, like fall in off the dock or do my strokes wrong.

"What about you, Lorelei?"

"I'm probably going to just hang around the farm, sketching and drawing all summer," I said. "It'll be fun!"

"What about you, Abril?" asked Corinne.

"Nothing really," Abril said. "I wish there was some kind of theater group in town. Dad says people used to put on plays in the town park. There's an outdoor stage there and the audience would sit on blankets on the hillside and watch." She sighed. "I wish they'd do something like that this summer. I'd love to perform in a play!"

My friend has a dramatic flair, that's for certain. She was the lead* in the little play that our school put on this winter, and she was really good. Unlike me, she doesn't seem to have a shy bone in

25

her body.

Then Abril jumped to her feet. "Hey, that's just given me an idea for something we can do right now! The other night I watched a funny movie about spies. In one scene, they all jumped from a cliff into a raging river and swam to safety. Let's reenact the scene, you guys. Come on, it will be amazing! We can do it right here in the barn."

We all listened as Abril outlined how we'd jump from the top of the haystack into piles of straw beneath and then pretend to swim to "shore." Carter and Corinne were swept away by Abril's enthusiasm*. Me? I was a little more cautious.

"Do you really think this is safe?" I protested.

"Lorelei, we've all done this before," said Abril, with her eyebrows raised. "You have too, right?"

Corinne put her hand on my arm. "Abril, if Lorelei doesn't want to jump, maybe she shouldn't. After all," Corinne hesitated, "she does tend to be a bit accident-prone. Remember her papier-mâché

26

project at school? How she ended up accidentally squashing it?"

"And that time she jumped off the swing in the playground and hurt her ankle and we had to carry her into class?" Carter chimed in.

I looked at my friends. I wasn't sure whether to feel good that they didn't want me to get hurt or upset that they thought I was klutzy.

"Oh come on, Lorelei," said Abril, laughing it off. "You'll be fine. We've all done it a million times, and this time, we'll all be spies leaping to safety!"

I could never resist Abril. I agreed, and one by one, we all did our jumps. It was fine and safe. Actually it was more than fine. It was fun…lots of fun!

"If only we had some sheets, we could pretend we were wearing parachutes," cried Abril, as she did another leap.

In a little while, Corinne and Carter's mom poked her head into the barn, telling them it was time to go.

After we said our goodbyes, I suddenly remembered something. "Abril," I said, "there might be some old sheets in the back of the barn! Maybe we can use them the next time we do hay bale jumping."

"Excellent!" Abril cried.

As we headed to look for them, Abril glanced at me. "Is there something bothering you, Lorelei?" she asked. "You seem a bit upset... worried maybe."

Only Abril, my best friend, would have guessed.

I told her about our family conversation last night, and about our worries for other small dairy farmers. She listened sympathetically.

"I just wish there was something I could do," I concluded.

A few seconds later, I spotted the sheets.

"Here they are!" I said. We began gathering them up and shaking the dust off.

"These will be great," said Abril. "But look what they were covering! It seems to be different types of old farm machinery."

"I wonder if these are farming tools that my grandparents or even my great-grandparents used," I said, examining the tools. "Look, there's a tractor, a plow…but what's this? Some kind of a freezer?"

"And this? It reminds me of the ice cube maker that's on our refrigerator," said Abril.

"That's strange," I said, puzzling over the two machines. "I wonder what these were for, and what they're doing here?"

Just then, Abril's older brother, Rodrigo, showed up. When Abril bikes over to our farm, Abril's parents usually send Rodrigo to bike home with her.

"Are you back there? Time to go, sis."

"Coming!" Abril called.

To me, she said, "Ask your Gran if she knows what these mystery machines were used for!" She winked. "And call me when you think of a plan for helping out the other farmers. If you need a hand putting it into action, I'm in!"

Chapter Four

ANSWER? ICE CREAM!

"Oh my goodness!" said Gran. We were all sitting at the dinner table, finishing our meal. I'd just told my family about the mysterious items that Abril and I had found in the old barn.

"You've discovered our ice cream maker and freezer!" said Gran. "Your dear grandpa and I bought that many years ago, Lorelei. We were going to make our very own ice cream with the milk from our cows. We planned to sell it to the local shops, just to bring in a little more money."

My dad nodded. "I remember," he said. "It was a really good idea."

"Then your grandpa got sick, and we had to put our plan on hold," Gran explained. "My, I'd forgotten all about it!"

Suddenly, I jumped to my feet. "Well, what

do you know, everyone! There's my big idea!"

Mom was puzzled. "What do you mean, Lorelei?"

"Ice cream!" exclaimed Joey. "I love ice cream!"

"Who doesn't love ice cream?" I asked. "So that's what we can do: make our own ice cream using the milk from our cows."

Gran grinned. "Make our own ice cream? What a fine idea!"

"Do you still remember how to use the ice cream machine, Mom?" asked Dad.

"Yes, sirree!" said Gran. "And I remember how much fun your father and I had, trying it out."

Mom smiled. "We can make a small amount of ice cream and sell it to the local stores, just like your granny and grandpa had planned, Lorelei. We can use the money to help out local farmers."

Thoughts were racing through my mind. I thought back to what my friends and I had talked about earlier—the town park and beach.

"Instead of selling ice cream to the stores," I said, "what if we sold it at the park in town this summer? It's right on the lake. That way, everyone would see with their own eyes how ice cream comes from the milk made on small farms like ours!"

"It would be a great way to spread the word about how important small farmers are," Gran said, enthusiastically. "Lots of people from town spend time there on the hot days, and there are many summer visitors, too."

"Lorelei, you could make a brochure* to give out to customers, telling them about small dairy farms. You can explain what we do and why what we do is important," said Dad. "You could include your own drawings. Some of your cow drawings, especially!"

I paused. *Show my drawings to strangers?* Then I nodded. *Maybe. For this really special cause...*

But then I frowned. "How will we get the ice cream to the park without it melting?" I asked.

"We can't just drive it there in our car and sell it from the trunk."

We all thought for a moment.

Mom grinned. "We'll get an ice cream truck! Gran, if you can help make the ice cream, I'll drive the truck to the park. Lorelei and I can sell the ice cream there together."

"Lorelei's too fumbly," Joey said, pouting. "What if she drops the cones?"

"Joey, don't be mean," said Mom, gently. She gave me a wink. We both knew my little brother was only saying that because he was feeling left out.

✦ ✦

Later that night, after Mom and Dad had both kissed me goodnight, I stayed awake for a while, doodling* and thinking about our plan. I sketched some ice cream cones and happy cow faces—Josephine's and Claudia's. I drew an ice cream truck with a long line of people, waiting to get cones.

But then I began to worry. I'm not too keen* on meeting new people. I've never actually met any of the kids that go to the school in town. Would I have to chit-chat with the customers? Mom is good at that. Abril is good at that kind of thing, too. She's extroverted* and likes being around new people. But not me. Maybe I wouldn't be friendly enough to sell ice cream.

I drew pictures of our barn and the milking machines. I drew my dad and Todd feeding the cows.

I really liked the idea of making a brochure to tell people about dairy farming and how important it is to keep our small farms running. But were my drawings really good enough to include? What if the customers laughed at them?

As I turned out the light and hugged my kitty-face pillow, I decided I'd have to think about it some more. There was still one more week of school and lots to do before I had to worry about ice cream customers!

Chapter Five

OOPS GO THE SCOOPS!

The next day was my favorite day of the week—Saturday! Mom said it was OK if Abril came over, so I called her right after breakfast. I told her everything that my family had talked about last night and our plans for making and selling ice cream.

"Do you want to come over and help me figure out more about how we can make this work?" I asked.

"I'll be there pronto*," she said. "My dad's just leaving to go to the feed store. He'll drop me off."

About ten minutes later, Abril knocked on the door.

The first thing we decided to do was to ask

Gran how ice cream is made from milk. Abril and I joined Gran on the couch as she explained the process.

She said that the fresh milk from our cows would be taken to a processing plant where it would be pasteurized* and homogenized*, as it always is.

"Usually our milk goes off from there to be bottled and sold," said Gran. "But now, some of it will be brought back here. We'll add eggs and sugar to the milk to make what's called a "base." We'll put the base into the batch freezer, which is one of the machines you two girls found in the barn, and we'll churn* it so it becomes light and fluffy as it freezes. We'll add ingredients to the base to make different flavors. Then we'll pop that in the storage freezer, which is the other machine you girls found. It'll freeze very, very quickly—and that's it! Homemade ice cream!"

"Hi, girls! Hi, Mom!" Dad peered through the open window at us. Joey was by his side. "Mom, can you give Joey and me a hand? It's time to dust off these ice cream machines and see if we can get them running!"

Gran took a final sip of tea and hurried away. Abril and I went to look for my mom. We found her doing paperwork at her desk.

"Mom, is it OK if we do a search on the Internet?" I asked. "We need to learn more about the cost of ingredients."

With Mom's permission, we spent an hour or so on the computer. We figured out how many eggs and how much sugar we'd need to make 10 gallons of ice cream. We also talked about what ingredients we could add to make different flavors, like raspberries and chocolate chips.

"You'll need lots of cones," said Abril.

"And paper cups with wooden spoons," I added.

In a while, Dad called us all to lunch. While we ate, he shared the good news that the ice cream machines were dusty but in good working order. Mom asked if Abril and I wanted to go into town with her and Joey to get some groceries.

"After shopping, we should probably do some hands-on research into ice cream cone prices," Mom suggested, trying to keep a straight face. "We may just be forced to buy several cones at the drive-through."

Of course, we agreed!

As we pulled into the grocery store parking lot, I noticed an art supply store across the street.

"Can we get some materials to make our brochures about dairy farming?" I asked.

"Great idea!" Mom said.

☙ ❧

After getting groceries, we all went to the art supply store. Abril and I looked around, and soon I saw the store clerk heading toward us. I felt awkward about talking to a stranger, and I hoped Mom would come over and tell him what we wanted. But when I looked nervously in her direction, she just nodded at me encouragingly.

Luckily, Abril spoke up and explained our project.

Abril is so outgoing and confident. If only I could be more like her...

"Abril, you're a star at talking to people you've never met," I told her, as we left the store with everything we needed. "How do you do it?"

"Ah, but you see, I'm in training! I was playing a role, just *acting* like a confident young lady!" she insisted. "And I was good, right?"

We were still laughing when we reached the car.

"Now, ice cream, ice cream," sang out Joey. "I scream for ice cream!"

"We're off!" said Mom.

We drove to the drive-through restaurant on the other side of town.

"Hmmm," suggested Mom, "maybe we should each order something different. Just to research a wider variety of offerings of course!"

We ended up with two cones, a cup of ice cream, and a sundae—and big smiles on our faces.

"Hey, Mom, can we eat our ice cream at the beachside park?" I asked. "That way we can check out where we'll be bringing our ice cream truck this summer."

We pulled up near Butterton Park and piled out of the car.

"How pretty it is here!" Mom exclaimed. "So many lovely trees!"

"And look. There's the old stage over there." Abril pointed to a large clearing where a wooden stage sat in a hollow*. "Dad calls it the "theater-in-the-round*." She sighed. "If only someone would put on a play there this summer."

Joey stared at the lake. "Sand! Water!" he exclaimed, grasping his sundae in both hands.

The sun sparkled on the blue water of the lake. *If only I had my paints! I'd love to capture the color and beauty of this park,* I thought.

I stood, gazing at the scene. Suddenly Joey hollered, "Lorelei, watch out!"

The ice cream, piled high on my cone, was teetering. Next thing I knew, it had toppled right off and splatted on the grass at my feet.

Joey was giggling, and so were six or seven

kids, all my age, kids I'd never seen before. They stood nearby, watching me. One boy held his stomach, like he couldn't stop laughing. A blond girl lifted her chin in the air, flipped back her hair, and turned away.

I'm sure I turned beet red. Then the kids climbed on their bikes and rode off.

"Here, ignore them. Have some of my ice cream," said Abril, handing me her ice cream cup.

But I could only stand there, holding my empty cone, scoops of strawberry and chocolate-swirl ice cream at my feet.

"Those kids might be our customers soon," I said to Abril, mortified*. "They're going to see me serving them ice cream! What will they think?"

"They won't even remember this," said Abril, "and neither should you."

Still, I couldn't move. But then Joey said, "Lorelei, can I put the ice cream you dropped onto my sundae?" He bent down to pick it up.

Mom shrieked, "No, Joey!" and everyone forgot about my fumble. Everyone except me, that is.

Chapter Six

SWEET STOP

"I hope we like it, I hope we like it," I chanted.

It was Tuesday evening of the final week of school. Mom had searched through the online* listings and found an ice cream truck for sale just a few towns away. Now, Mom, Dad, Gran, Joey and I were on our way to check it out.

Gran, our navigator*, pointed to the address on a mailbox by the side of the road. "Here we are. This must be it."

Dad drove down a long driveway.

"There it is! The ice cream truck!" cried Joey, as we all saw the light blue truck parked beside the farmhouse.

I crossed my fingers. *I hope it's just what we want.*

We piled out of the car and a man came out to greet us. Joey's eyes grew wide. "Lorelei," he whispered to me. "It's Santa Claus!"

"Maybe," I agreed, with a smile. With his bushy white beard, twinkling eyes and large belly, the man did look a lot like Santa.

"Hello, hello," the man said, extending his hand. "I'm Sal Frosty."

Mom introduced us all. Sal shook our hands, even Joey's and mine.

"Come along. I'll give you a tour of Sweet Stop," he suggested, leading us over to his truck. "That's what I call her. I sold ice cream in her on weekends through the summer months. I've decided to retire, but I'll miss my Sweet Stop, for sure."

Sal pointed to the big side window. "The customers lined up there. The window slides open, and I served the ice cream through it."

He opened the truck's back door, and we all climbed in.

"Wow!" gasped Joey.

There was a long counter with trays for setting out all the different flavors of ice cream. There was a freezer, an ice cream cup dispenser on the wall, a sink for washing up and a bell to ring for service. There was a shelf with napkin and straw holders on it.

Sal pointed to several unopened boxes. "Here are some napkins, cups, straws, wooden spoons, and even some sprinkles, to get you started."

Mom moved into the cab and sat down in the driver's seat. She put her feet on each of the pedals and held the steering wheel.

"Sweet Stop is quite sweet to drive," said Sal, giving the side of the truck an affectionate pat. "She never gave me a problem."

"What's this, Mr. Frosty?" asked Joey, as he pointed to a switch on the wall.

"Try it," said Sal.

Joey flipped it on, and suddenly, music filled the air.

Gran was busily examining a pink sandwich board that was also a chalkboard. "Lorelei, dear, you can draw pictures of the items you are selling on this and set it up outside the truck each day."

I was so excited. Everything about the truck seemed just right. I gave Mom and Dad a thumbs-up, and so did Joey and Gran. Mom and Dad nodded at each other.

Mom said to Sal, "We'd like to make an offer on your truck."

"Wonderful!" said Sal, beaming. "But first, may I ask why your family decided to buy an ice cream truck?"

Gran explained that we'd be making the ice cream ourselves, using the milk from our own dairy farm cows, but that our main goal was to raise money and awareness about other small dairy farms.

When Sal heard that, he was quiet for a moment. Then he took my parents aside.

Soon, all three of them were back, grinning.

"Mr. Frosty is offering us a discount on the truck," Mom announced. "It's very generous of him. And we've insisted that Mr. Frosty have all the milk and ice cream he wants from our dairy—for life!"

"Ya-hoo!" I cried. Our summer project had begun!

        ✤ ✤

When I got home from school the next day, Gran called me into the kitchen.

"Lorelei, dear," she said, "early this morning, some of our milk was delivered back to us from the dairy. I made an ice cream base and it's been in the freezer all day. Shall we try making some different flavors?"

"Yes!" I said, enthusiastically.

"I thought we could start with adding vanilla," said Gran. She looked at me inquiringly. "Everyone likes vanilla ice cream, right?"

"Um, OK, Gran," I said, slowly. "But... isn't that a bit boring? All that...white? Maybe our customers would like more colorful ice cream cones!"

Gran smiled. "Perhaps."

I opened the refrigerator and pulled out some strawberries, some blueberries and a bag of chocolate chips. "Let's try these!" I suggested.

"Alright," said Gran. We began mixing.

"And we'll have lots of different toppings." I said. "Chocolate sprinkles, colored sprinkles, candies…and maybe some syrups, too. That way our customers can choose what to put on top."

"They'll have lots of fun," said Gran. "How are the brochures coming along?"

I told Gran that I'd finished the wording for them and that I was still making the drawings.

"Would you read what I've written and let me know what you think?" I asked. "I'm not sure if it's good enough yet."

"I'd be happy to," said Gran. "We'll do that after dinner."

❦ ❦

As I turned off my bedside light that night, I felt good. Gran had helped me with the brochure and the words were now just right. I was almost done with the drawings. When they were finished, and placed with the words, we could get them printed and ready for the weekend. That's when we'd really begin our ice cream adventure.

I was excited, but I was still worried about having to talk to our customers—all those people I'd never met before. I remembered the kids who laughed at me in the park, and I remembered how Abril had said not to worry.

I sighed. Abril was so good with people, even strangers. *She'd be much better at serving ice cream than I'd be,* I thought.

Suddenly, I jumped out of bed and ran downstairs. Mom and Dad were in the living room, having a cup of tea and reading.

"Mom, can Abril help out in the ice cream truck?" I asked. "She doesn't have any summer plans. She wants to do some acting, so maybe she'd like a summer role as an ice cream seller!"

Mom and Dad laughed.

"Sure," Mom said. "If it's OK with her parents, of course she's welcome to help us. Every single day, if she'd like!"

I gave Mom a kiss, and I gave Dad one, too. Then I scooted back to bed. Summer was going to be fun!

Chapter Seven

ICE CREAM ON THE BRAIN

It was the last day of school. After wishing Mrs. Fisher a happy summer, I paused on the steps of the school bus. "See you tomorrow, Abril," I called over my shoulder. "Our first day of the ice cream project!"

As I walked quickly up the long lane toward our house, I watched the green corn stalks sway in the gentle breeze. The clouds in the sky reminded me of scoops of ice cream.

I definitely had ice cream on the brain*. After school over the last two days, Gran and I had made several buckets of base ice cream. Today, we were adding ingredients to make two different flavors, which Mom, Abril and I would sell tomorrow.

I made a quick visit to the cows after school. I missed seeing them every day. Then, full of anticipation, I hurried into the kitchen, where Gran had prepared a work space.

"Here I am, Gran!" I cried.

"Oh good, Lorelei," she answered. "I have everything ready."

I tied my hair back, washed my hands and got to work.

Together, Gran and I added bananas and a little lemon to one bucket of base ice cream to make banana ice cream. We added cocoa and semi-sweet chocolate chips to another bucket of base ice cream to make chocolate ice cream. And to the final bucket we only added vanilla. Gran and I agreed that vanilla ice cream would be very popular, especially with all the toppings that Sal had given us.

Just then, Mom came in. "Good news, team," she announced. "I got the permit for the truck, which means we have permission to set up in the park and sell our ice cream there.

"Oh, and look at these!" She held up three aprons. They were decorated with colorful stars...

and our names!

"One for me, one for you and one for Abril," she said. There was a hat and a striped bow tie for Abril and me, too.

Mom had also bought ice cream scoops, jars of sprinkles in many different colors, cones and more cups, spoons and napkins.

"And look," she said, as she opened a bag and pulled out a box. "I had Lorelei's brochures printed out in town. They look terrific! We have enough here to give one to each customer all summer!"

"Hurray! We're all set for tomorrow," I said, with a grin.

꒰꒱ ꒰꒱

"I'd like to try a scoop of banana ice cream please," said the elderly man. His wife pointed to the vanilla and nudged him. "And one vanilla for my wife," he added.

"Coming right up," said Mom. She turned to Abril and me. "Girls, could you prepare the cones for our very first customers, please?"

It was Saturday morning. Mom, Abril and I had loaded up the truck and set up in the park.

I drew our featured flavors of ice cream on the pink sandwich board. Then I carefully added the name "Sweet Stop" to the chalkboard on the side of the truck. We put on our aprons, placed the napkins and straws in their holders and arranged all the sprinkle jars.

Finally, I switched on Sweet Stop's cheerful tune to let everyone know that the ice cream truck was here.

Luckily, most of the people in the park at that hour were parents with toddlers, or older people—playing chess, walking their dogs or just relaxing on benches.

"Here you go!" Abril said, handing each of our first two customers a cone. I also handed them a brochure, and then Abril gave a brief, but passionate*, explanation about why dairy farms are important.

"This ice cream is made from milk that

comes from a local farm," she said. "My friend Lorelei's dairy farm!"

The man and woman nodded, impressed.

"We'll read this carefully," said the woman.

I watched as more and more families and kids my age arrived in the park, but I was relieved when none of the kids came over to our truck. They swam in the lake, played ball on the beach and rode their bikes around.

Several more customers wandered over throughout the afternoon, and we served them all without mishap*. Once, while Abril was helping Mom in the back of the truck, I got up the nerve* to chat with a customer about dairy farms.

"Oh my, what cute drawings," she said, looking at the brochure.

Sal Frosty even showed up. "Seems like Sweet Stop is working out fine for you," he said, patting the truck.

"She sure is!" I said.

"She's easy to drive and she has everything we need inside," Mom said.

Abril and I put a scoop of each of our three flavors of the week in a special cup for Sal. "On the house, of course," I told him, presenting him with the treat.

Shortly after, Abril said, "Look!" A whole group of kids around our age were heading toward the theater-in-the-round. "I wonder what they're doing. Come on, Lorelei. Let's go and find out."

"No," I said, quickly. "You go, if you want. I think I'd better stay here and help Mom."

"Sure?" Abril asked, uncertainly, but I gave a quick nod.

When she returned a while later, she rushed inside and gave me an excited hug.

"Lorelei, you'll never guess!" she said. "Turns out all those kids are working on a play this summer for a regional competition*. The play has to be overseen by adults—but it must be completely produced and performed by children. All the plays, including this one, will be performed at the end of the summer and judged."

Abril's eyes were shining. "Doesn't that

sound fantastic?"

I didn't say anything.

"And Nina—that's one of the girls—she invited me to try out for a part! I'm going to ask my parents if I can. Nina says almost everyone who tries out will get a part. You should do it too, Lorelei!" She grasped my arm. "We could do it together!"

"Abril, you know it's not really my…thing," I said, slowly. "Acting, memorizing lines…."

"But Lorelei, it would be so great if we could do it together," Abril said.

I swallowed. "Well, I don't think so. That's not for me. But we do have this," I reminded her. "We are serving ice cream together all summer, aren't we?"

I wasn't sure how this was going to work out. *Is she saying she doesn't want to help out with the ice cream truck anymore? What about all our plans?* I worried.

I could tell Abril was thinking.

"Lorelei, would you be OK with this?" she

asked. "I could help out here in the mornings, and then work on the play with Nina—and all the town kids—in the afternoon. If my parents say OK, and I get the part, that is. Would that be alright?"

I shrugged. "I guess so," I said, although I wasn't exactly sure if it was OK with me or not. I looked down at the countertop and began wiping it with a dish rag.

"Oh yay! You're such a cool friend, Lorelei." Abril pulled a piece of paper out of her pocket. "Nina's phone number," she said. "She asked me to call her tonight and let her know what my parents say."

There wasn't one tiny bit of ice cream left on the countertop, but I scrubbed even harder at it. Abril loved performing and so did Nina. *Was there any chance Abril would end up liking this Nina girl more than she liked me?*

Chapter Eight

THAT WAS NINA?

The next day, Mom, Abril and I loaded up the truck with fresh ice cream and drove to the park. Just like the day before, the customers in the morning were mainly elderly people and parents with small children. Abril couldn't stop smiling at everyone. She'd told me first thing that her parents said she could try out for the play.

I was hoping we'd make it through the day again without any of the town kids coming over, but this time, a whole group of them arrived around noon. Of course, luck was against me. Mom had just asked Abril to stack the cups, cones and napkins in the back, so it was up to me to help out.

"What would you like?" I nervously asked the first boy in line. The others behind him were shoving one another playfully, and yelling, "Hey, hurry up, Greg. You're holding up the line."

"Chocolate cone, two scoops," he said to me.

"We'll be here all day," one of the girls complained.

I felt more frazzled*. "Mom, can you or Abril help me?" I called.

"Be right there, honey," she replied.

I managed to serve him his cone, and also prepared cones for the next two customers, but then a girl with blond hair was standing at the order window.

"Banana, I guess," she said, with a sigh, flipping her hair back, "with chocolate sprinkles."

I know that hair flip! She was the girl who had put her chin in the air and turned away when I dropped my cone in the park. I was distracted, and knocked over the bag of chocolate sprinkles, which I'd forgotten to put away after filling the shaker. They all began to fall into the big dish of small candy toppings.

As I reached out to catch that bag, I knocked over the bag of colored sprinkles, which I'd also forgotten to put away. All those sprinkles also cascaded into the dish of candies!

I stood there, frozen. Then I held out the cone to the girl so she could put on her toppings.

"But I asked for chocolate sprinkles! I don't want this…this mixed-up mess," she said, frowning at the colorful combination in the candy bowl.

I showed her the empty sprinkle bags. "I'm so sorry, but we don't have anything else to offer at the moment," I said. "You'll have to take all or nothing."

"Well, then, I pick nothing. I don't even want the cone now," the girl said, flipping her hair back again. She stalked away.

"Nina, don't be so silly," called the boy who was next in line. He turned to me and shook his head. "Actresses. They can seem a bit stuck up sometimes. But Nina's OK once you get to know her."

Nina? That was Nina? I swallowed hard.

Just then, Mom hurried over to help out. When she saw the mess I had made, she frowned, but the boy cheerfully used the spoon to pour the new combination topping onto his ice cream. Still, I was feeling bad, especially when Abril reminded us that it was time for her audition*. I only managed to give her a halfhearted* smile.

"Good luck," Mom called, as Abril hurried away.

By then, most of the other kids who had been lined up had left also, probably heading off to the auditions. Mom was staring at the big bowl of mixed toppings, with her arms crossed.

"I guess Joey must be right," I said. "I am a fumblebumbler."

Mom glanced at me. Then she stopped frowning.

"Maybe, but that last customer seemed to like your new concoction*," said Mom. She dipped a spoon into the bowl of mixed toppings and put the heaping spoonful into her mouth. "Yum! I think that's my new favorite," she said, grinning. "I know, let's name it 'Fumblebumbler Fave'!"

I giggled. "Really?"

"Really," said Mom. She scooped some ice cream into a cup, covered it in sprinkles and handed it to me. "Here, give it a try. I think you've just created a masterpiece!"

We ended up sharing the treat. Afterwards, I erased the list of three toppings on the sandwich board, and I wrote in the one new special topping:

Fumblebumbler Fave

No way am I going to let one little fumble get me down, I decided. *No way is Nina going to ruin my summer project or my friendship with my best friend.*

When Abril arrived back at Sweet Stop later in the afternoon, she had great news.

"I got a big part in the play!" she exclaimed.

I cried, "Congratulations!" and gave her a big hug. I was sure things were all going to work out.

Chapter Nine

A SPECIAL TIME

I sighed happily. It was the end of July. Our ice cream truck had been doing a fantastic business! We were earning lots of money to share with other dairy farmer families and we were spreading the word about the importance of small dairy farms.

My family had a good routine going. Gran and I made ice cream every night, and sometimes Joey helped. Dad and Todd took care of our cows. Mom, Abril and I went to the park each day and served ice cream. When there weren't too many customers, Mom sat in the shade of the trees. She caught up on her accounting work on her laptop computer, or she read a book.

I created more artwork. Sometimes I used my pastels. I loved capturing the greens of the leaves and the different shades of blue in the lake. Or I

did caricatures of our customers. I chose one of their features and exaggerated it with a few pencil strokes. Sometimes it was a long nose or a bald head. Sometimes it was the shape of someone's eyes or mouth. Then I added some color to give the drawing pizzazz*!

Abril would work on memorizing her lines for the play and sometimes I helped her. She said everyone was working hard. Some kids were creating costumes and others were making the props for the set. There was even one boy operating the lights. The play was going to be performed at twilight at the end of the summer, so having just the right lighting was important.

"I think the play will be good, Lorelei," Abril told me. "Wouldn't it be great if we won the competition? You have to promise to come and watch."

"Of course I'll come!" I told her. "Wild horses couldn't keep me away*."

Abril would head over to the theater-in-the-round for the last half of the afternoon to rehearse with Nina and the other kids. I tried not to feel too bad about her spending so much time with them.

Just because she has a new friend that shares her interest in acting, it doesn't mean that Abril and I aren't still best friends. That's what I kept telling myself anyway.

And during that part of the day, Mom and I would continue to serve ice cream together. It was actually nice to have some time alone with Mom.

One day, she asked if I was feeling more comfortable serving ice cream to the town kids. I told her yes, but I wasn't really sure if I was or not.

Another day she told me stories about when I was little. And then the next day she told me stories about when *she* was little.

Sometimes I showed her my drawings, or she'd describe the plot* of one of the books she was reading.

It was turning out to be a special time for the two of us.

Chapter Ten

LOSING A BEST FRIEND?

"I can't believe the play is this Saturday. It's only three days away!" Abril said.

It was the final week of August. We were preparing ice cream cups for a family of four.

"I'm a bit nervous, but Nina says..." Abril stopped speaking. I watched as she scooped a ball of peach ice cream into a cup.

I'd been trying not to show Abril that her new friendship with Nina worried me, but I guess it had been more obvious than I realized. I felt bad. *I should have more confidence in Abril*, I thought.

"Nina says what?" I asked, cheerfully, after we had handed over four cups of ice cream, along with a brochure, to the waiting family.

"Nina says I'll be fine," Abril said.

"That's what I was going to say, too," I said

firmly. "Nina is right."

Abril sent me a grateful look. But then she suddenly turned away. A small group of the town kids were at the truck window, joking and chatting.

"Hello! Have you decided what you'd like?" Mom asked them, with a bright smile. To me, she said, "Lorelei, can you come and give me a hand?"

As I stepped up to the counter to help Mom take the orders, Abril said, "I'll be right back."

Mom and I were soon busy scooping and serving. When we were done, I suddenly realized that Abril was there, under the trees, and Nina was there, too. I hadn't noticed her. She hadn't ordered ice cream. Perhaps she'd just come to say hi to Abril.

But wait. *Nina was looking upset! And... oh no! Abril was holding my sketchbook of caricatures. It was open, and Nina was looking at it....*

I had a sinking feeling. I'd done caricatures of strangers in the park and of people in my own family, but I'd also done some caricatures of some of the theater kids, including Nina. For fun.

"Mom, I'll be right back," I told her. I hurried out of the truck and over to the girls, but I stopped before they saw me. They were talking about me.

"You said that you thought Lorelei's drawings on the chalkboard and the sandwich board were good. I wanted you to see how good her caricatures are, too," I heard Abril say to Nina. "Lorelei is really talented."

"But look at the way she's drawn me!" Nina replied. "With my nose up in the air. I look...so snobby."

"Nina, the point of a caricature is to exaggerate some part of you. It's all in fun!" Abril said. She flipped the page and showed another drawing to Nina. "Look, Lorelei drew a caricature of me, too. See! She drew me with my ears really exaggerated. I'm her friend—but she made me look like an elephant! Isn't it funny?"

"It is," said Nina, giggling.

Abril put her arm around Nina's shoulders. "Now look again at the one she did of you." She turned the page back. "Well?"

"Hmm, I see what you mean," said Nina, reluctantly*. "Yes, I guess it is funny, even if she did make me look snobby."

"I'm sure you and Lorelei would like each other if the two of you got to know each other. If you just gave each other a chance," Abril reassured her.

᷍ ᷍

"And so that's what happened," I told Gran, later than night. I had just described the conversation I'd overheard between Abril and Nina. "Gran," I said, my voice quivering, "I'm worried that I might be losing my best friend."

Gran patted my hand. "Darling Lorelei, it's nice for Abril to have a new friend. It doesn't mean she can't still be your best friend, too."

I nodded. She was right. I just needed to hear someone say it out loud, I guess.

But there was something else bothering me.

"Gran, I can't stop thinking about the families that may have to move away if they can't afford to keep their farms," I said. "We're giving out so many brochures at the ice cream truck. But how do we know that it will make a difference?"

"Well, honey," she said, patting my hand again, "we don't know. Not for certain. But it might. And you're trying your best to make a difference." She smiled. "I'm proud of you."

I smiled back. Gran always manages to cheer me up.

Before I knew it, it was Saturday morning. School would start in a few days. Mom said she had to catch up on her accounting work, so today would be our very last day selling ice cream this summer.

I'd miss it. But it also meant that the play was tonight, and after today, Abril wouldn't be spending as much time with Nina. I felt guilty being happy about that, but I hoped it meant my friendship with Abril would go back to normal.

The phone rang. "Lorelei, I can't come with you and your mom today," Abril told me. "We have a special all-day practice for the play. I forgot to tell you yesterday. I'll try to come by and say hello, though," she assured me. "I know it's the last day for Sweet Stop!"

I swallowed hard. I'd been looking forward to spending this last day of the ice cream project with Abril. "OK, no problem," I told her lightly.

Gran and Joey helped Mom and me load up the truck for the last time.

"Raspberry ice cream, maple ice cream and vanilla ice cream for today," Gran said.

"And of course, we have the colored sprinkles, the chocolate sprinkles, the candies and the Fumblebumbler Fave toppings!" said Mom.

We headed to the park and set up for the day. All morning, customers kept coming by and saying how much they'd miss us, and thanking us for the information about small dairy farms.

One woman said she'd started a petition

for people in the community to sign, asking our governor* to take action to protect small dairy farms.

A man told us he had started a website to help spread more information about dairy farming.

It felt strange not to have Abril there, and I missed her. I tried to focus on hoping that her final rehearsal at the theater-in-the-round was going well.

The day zipped by. It was only when we were packing up to leave that I realized Abril hadn't come by. *Did it mean...?*

No. No, it has nothing to do with our friendship, I told myself sternly*. *Abril is working hard for tonight, and she just didn't have time to say goodbye to Sweet Stop.*

Chapter Eleven

SHOW TIME!

A few hours later, Dad, Mom, Gran, Joey and I were finding seats on the hillside. There was a large crowd of people gathered to watch the play. I recognized lots of farming families and many kids from my school. Abril's parents and her brother were there, of course.

I was just sitting down on the grass when Abril came running up to me. Her face was red, and she looked like she might cry.

"Lorelei, the boy who normally does the lights is sick and he can't do his job tonight. We just found out. The other kids in the show are too busy to do the lights, but we can't perform without them. It will just be too dark for the audience to see anything!" Abril spoke quickly, without taking a breath. "We don't know who we can ask to help.

It has to be another kid—that's one of the rules for the competition."

I looked around. "Well, some of our other friends are here from school," I told her. "Look, there's Corinne. And I saw Carter earlier."

Abril grabbed my arm. "Lorelei, you're the one. I know you can help us."

"Me?" I said, surprised. "But I don't know anything about lights! And…"

What if I make a mistake? What if I don't manage to hit the right switch? Doing lighting probably needs coordination. And my own brother calls me a fumblebumbler!

That's what I wanted to say.

But I bit my tongue*. Here was my friend—my best friend—and she was asking for my help.

Abril stared at me, biting her lip.

I took a deep breath. "OK," I nodded. "If you think I can do it, if you really need me to do the lights, I'll help as best I can."

Her face broke into a huge grin. "Oh, Lorelei. Thank you!" she said, and right then I felt the happiest I'd felt all summer.

Abril and I quickly explained to my family what was happening, and I hurried after her toward the stage.

I held my breath as I approached the other kids. They were dressed in their costumes and ready to hit the stage. *What would they think?* Most of them had seen me drop my ice cream cone in the park, but it was so long ago…maybe they'd forgotten.

But what about the topping fiasco*? I wondered. *And what about Nina? She'd been so upset when she saw my caricature of her. Had she spread the word that I was mean and not to be trusted?*

To my relief, when the other kids saw me and Abril called out, "She'll do it!" they looked pleased.

"They know I don't know anything about stage lighting, right?" I asked Abril, worried.

"Yup," said Abril. "And they also know that you're an artist—and have a great eye for

83

color and light."

I nodded. "OK. I hope I can manage."

From behind me, I heard a girl say, "I'm sure you'll be fine."

It was Nina. *Nina!* I couldn't believe it.

She took a deep breath. "I'm sorry I've been snobby with you, Lorelei. It's just… you're such a good artist, and you've been Abril's friend for so long…" Nina paused. "I guess I was a bit jealous of you, and I'm sorry I haven't been very nice."

I stared at her, speechless.

"Anyway, we've all worked really hard on our play, and we all really want to perform it tonight," said Nina. "Abril says you'll be great at doing the lighting—and well, you two are best friends, and so I'm sure she must be right!"

We're best friends? Nina called Abril and me best friends!

Suddenly my nerves vanished.

An older boy came over to us.

"I'm Clive, the stage manager. Let me give you a quick run-through of what you need to do tonight, Lorelei. I know a little about the lighting. We're not expecting you to do anything more than keep the stage bright enough for the audience to be able to see what's going on.

"Nothing fancy. No crazy effects or spotlighting, so don't worry. You can do it all with just this one switch, to be on the safe side. That way, you can't make any mistakes," Clive reassured me.

"Sure thing," I said. As I hurried off with him, Abril gave me a thumbs-up, and even Nina smiled at me encouragingly.

❧ ☙

After the play was announced, the actors took their places. As darkness fell on the park, I slowly moved the switch up, and the stage slowly filled with white light. The audience applauded, the actors began speaking their lines, and everything seemed to be going well.

All I had to do was watch and read along with the script, and then, when the first act was

over, turn down the lights.

Abril was performing brilliantly. She hadn't forgotten a single word of her lines. Some of the other actors had to be prompted, but no one seemed to mind too much. They were mostly having fun. I was fascinated, watching the action onstage.

Suddenly, one of the actors had to exit right past where I was standing. I moved quickly to slide out of the way, and I slipped. I scrambled to avoid falling—and accidentally hit a whole row of switches on the lighting box. Everyone watching from the hillside gasped as the stage was bathed in a full array of lights.

Oh no! Now I've done it! I held my breath and stared with dismay* at the actors, who were surprised by the sudden rainbow of colors. But they quickly continued on with their lines.

I realized that the actors were pleased and the gasps from the audience were ones of delight, not horror. *Phew!* Happily the lights had all gone on during a dramatic scene, so they were perfect!

It was so much fun seeing the whole stage lit

up in color! I took a closer look at the light box. Each light was labeled with its color and position.

What if I take a chance, I thought, *and try to create some more special lighting effects? What if it actually helps Abril and the other kids win the competition?*

I'd read the play many times through while I was helping Abril learn her lines, so I had an idea of when the scenes were supposed to be sad and slow-moving, or upbeat and exciting. I decided to experiment.

It made me so happy, adding and subtracting colors to fit the scenes. It was like using my pastels! And I didn't make any more fumblebumbler-y goofs. The play went off without a hitch. Abril, of course, was the best. But Nina was good, too. And she didn't even flip her hair once!

When the performance was over, the actors all took a bow. The audience stood up and applauded. Nina and Abril asked everyone else who had helped to come onto the stage, including the stage manager, the set builders, the costume makers—and me! Abril waved me over to stand between her and Nina, and we all took a bow together.

Then a woman holding a notebook stepped up onto the stage.

"The judge," Abril whispered.

"Thank you all for being part of this competition," the woman said. "I'm so impressed with how hard you've worked to create this wonderful performance. The acting, the costumes, the set—it was all terrific.

"I'm sorry to tell you that you did not win the competition." There were a few groans of disappointment. "However you should be very proud of yourselves, and I hope you decide to compete again next year."

After everyone clapped, she went on, "And I'd like to add that I was especially impressed with the creative and original lighting!"

Everyone clapped again, and then both Abril and Nina, grinning at me, insisted that I step forward for a special bow. I could hardly believe it!

Chapter Twelve

FUMBLEBUMBLER FAVE, OF COURSE!

"Do we really go back to school tomorrow, Abril?" I asked. Abril had joined my family for Sunday night dinner, and she and I had just finished clearing the dining room table.

"Yup," said Abril, sitting down again next to me. "This summer has just zoomed by, hasn't it? What a summer it's been!"

"Well, you girls really accomplished a lot," said Gran.

"You certainly did," said Mom. She held out an envelope. "And maybe now is a good time to give you this, Lorelei. It's from the dairy farm association. It's addressed to our family, but really meant for you."

Quickly, I opened the letter and began to read it silently to myself. Then my eyes widened, and I began to read aloud.

"We would like to thank you for your donation, Lorelei, and for helping spread the word about the importance of small dairy farms. We also enjoyed seeing the many drawings and caricatures of cows which your mother sent along to us."

I shot a surprised look at Mom.

"Read on," she urged me, smiling.

"We hope you will consider drawing some cows for our newsletter which we send out electronically to our members," I read. "We would be pleased to pay you a small fee for your work."

I looked up. "Wow!"

"Nice one, Lorelei," said Joey. "Guess you're not just a fumblebumbler after all!"

"Of course she's not, Joey," said Dad. "She makes some mistakes, like we all do, but she's also a very talented artist!"

"Well done, darling," said Mom.

"You'll do it, right?" said Abril, with a wink. "Your first professional gig*!"

"Of course I will!" I cried, enthusiastically. "But I don't want them to pay me." I looked at Gran.

"Do you think I can ask them to keep the money, to use for their organization?"

Gran nodded. "I'm quite sure they'll consider that a very generous offer." She stood up. "Ready for dessert now?"

"Is it OK if Abril and I run out to the barn for a minute, just to say good night to the cows?" I asked. "I've hardly been able to spend any time with them this summer."

❧ ❧

"Hello Delilah, and Bluebell and Clover," I said, as Abril and I gazed over the fence at the cows.

"I still don't know how you can tell them all apart," Abril said, admiringly. "But you know, that's one of your special gifts. That, and your amazing love of color and your talent for drawing and painting. Oh, and for doing lighting for plays!"

I laughed. "Thanks. But what about you? You were so great in the play. You're a terrific actress, and you love it so much." I turned and looked at Abril. "Do you think it matters that we have such different interests—and such different talents?"

"You're kidding, right?" Abril stared at me. "We've always been this way, always with our own separate passions, right?"

"Right," I agreed.

"And that's OK. It may mean we end up doing different things and following separate paths. But we've always been best friends, and I know we always will be. We have fun together, we care about each other and we care about the same big things— the important things," she said.

I felt a warm glow deep down.

"I guess it's kind of like that for us farm kids and the town kids," I said. "We might seem really different from one another, but maybe we care about the same big things."

"Right. Like making sure families can stay on their farms," said Abril.

"And putting on local plays with great actors and amazing lighting!" I said.

"And eating delicious homemade ice cream!" Abril laughed.

Just then, we heard Gran calling from the front porch. "Come on in, girls! Guess what's for dessert? Ice cream, made from our own milk! And for the topping? Fumblebumbler Fave, of course!"

I yelled, "Coming, Gran!" and my best friend and I ran back to the house together to share some very special ice cream.

Glossary

Many words have more than one meaning. Here are the definitions of words marked with this symbol * (an asterisk) as they are used in this story.

accounting: *keeping track of money spent and earned*

agricultural management: *the running of farms, including raising animals or growing crops*

audition: *a tryout for a role as an actor, singer or dancer*

"bit my tongue": *tried hard not to say something*

brochure: *a small booklet with pictures and information about a particular thing*

churn: *to stir or mix*

concoction: *food or drink made by mixing together several ingredients*

consultant: *a person who is paid to give advice to businesses*

criticizing: *finding fault with*

dismay: *a feeling of being worried or upset*

doodling: *drawing while thinking of something else*

eavesdrop: *secretly overhear a private conversation*

enthusiasm: *excitement*

exaggerates: *makes something seem larger and funnier than it really is*

extroverted: *outgoing*

fiasco: *a total failure, a big flop*

frazzled: *very upset*

gig: *a job that lasts a short time*

governor: *the leader of a state in the United States*

graze: *feed on grass*

halfhearted: *showing very little interest or excitement*

heritage: *traditions and history of a group of people*

hollow: *an area surrounded by small hills*

homogenized (milk): *mixed thoroughly so that the cream will not separate and float on the top*

keen, as in "keen on": *excited about*

lead: *the main actor*

lowed: *made a deep moo-ing sound*

mishap: *a small mistake*

mortified: *embarrassed or humiliated*

navigator: *a person who finds the way to a place*

nerve, as in "got up the nerve": *had courage to get through a difficult situation*

online: *on the Internet*

"on the brain": *unable to stop thinking something*

passionate: *with strong emotion*

pastel, as in "pastel colors": *pale or light*

pastels: *crayon-like chalks used for drawing*

pasteurized (milk): *heated to a high temperature to kill harmful germs*

pasture: *a large area of farmland where grass grows*

pizzazz: *extra-special style*

plot: *a series of events that make up the story in a book*

pronto: *right away*

red-winged blackbird: *a bird known for the patch of red on the wings of the male*

reassuringly: *in a way that makes someone feel less afraid*

regional competition: *a contest or challenge among groups or teams from a certain area*

reluctantly: *doing or saying something without really wanting to*

resourceful: *able to find solutions to problems*

sternly: *strictly or seriously*

theater-in-the-round: *a theater space with a stage in the middle that the audience sits around*

unique: *not like any other*

vet: *abbreviation for veterinarian, an animal doctor*

"wild horses couldn't keep me away": *expression meaning nothing could keep the person away*

Free The Children

The Power of a Girl

For every *Our Generation®* product you buy, a portion of sales goes to Free The Children's Power of a Girl Initiative to help provide girls in developing countries an education—the most powerful tool in the world for escaping poverty.

Did you know that out of the millions of children who aren't in school, 70% of them are girls? In developing communities around the world, many girls can't go to school. Usually it's because there's no school available or because their responsibilities to family (farming, earning an income, walking hours each day for water) prevent it.

Over the past two years, Free The Children has had incredible success with its Year of Water and Year of Education initiatives, providing 100,000 people with clean water for life and building 200 classrooms for overseas communities. This year, they celebrate the Year of Empowerment, focusing on supporting alternative income projects for sustainable development.

The most incredible part is that most of Free The Children's funding comes from kids just like you, holding lemonade stands, bake sales, penny drives, walkathons and more.

Just by buying an *Our Generation* product you have helped change the world, and you are powerful (beyond belief!) to help even more.

If you want to find out more, visit:
www.ogdolls.com/free-the-children

FREE THE CHILDREN
children helping children through education

Free The Children provided the factual information pertaining to their organization. Free The Children is a 501c3 organization.

this is **our** story

We are an extraordinary generation of girls. And have we got a story to tell.

Our Generation® is unlike any that has come before. We're helping our families learn to recycle, holding bake sales to support charities, and holding penny drives to build homes for orphaned children in Haiti. We're helping our little sisters learn to read and even making sure the new kid at school has a place to sit in the cafeteria.

All that and we still find time to play hopscotch and hockey. To climb trees, do cartwheels all the way down the block and laugh with our friends until milk comes out of our noses. You know, to be kids.

Will we have a big impact on the world? We already have. What's ahead for us? What's ahead for the world? We have no idea. We're too busy grabbing and holding on to the joy that is today.

Yep. This is our time. This is our story.

www.ogdolls.com

Lorelei and Gran are lucky! They can use the milk from the cows on their dairy farm to make homemade ice cream. But you don't have to live on a farm to make your own ice cream. You can use milk or cream that you buy at the store. Give it a try!

Lorelei's grandmother helped her to make ice cream. Ask an adult to help you, too!

Make Your Own Ice Cream

Materials You Will Need:
1 gallon-size and 1 pint-size plastic bag (sealable)
3 cups of crushed ice
6 tablespoons of salt (You can use any kind of salt, including table salt, but kosher salt or rock salt works best.)
large bowl, small bowl and stirring spoon
towel or oven mitts

Ingredients For Ice Cream:
$\frac{1}{2}$ cup of any kind of milk or cream (Note: the more fat in the milk or cream, the thicker and creamier your ice cream will be!)
1 tablespoon of sugar
$\frac{1}{4}$ teaspoon of vanilla
optional: additional ingredients to flavor or decorate the ice cream, such as pieces of fruit, chocolate or butterscotch chips, chocolate or maple syrup, sprinkles or candies

1. Gather your ingredients and materials. Put ice into the large plastic bag until it is half full. Add the salt. Stir until the ice and salt are mixed well.

2. Put milk or cream, sugar, and vanilla into a bowl. Mix well. Pour into the small plastic bag. Try to push as much air out of the bag as possible. Seal the bag tightly.

3. Put the small bag into the large bag. Make sure it is completely covered in ice. Then seal the large bag tightly.

4. Now shake, shake, shake the bag! The bag might get slippery so you may want to hold it with a towel or with your oven mitts on. But whatever you do, keep on shaking!

5. Have you kept up the shaking for about five to seven minutes? Open the large bag and take out the smaller bag. Now scoop out the vanilla ice cream into a small bowl.

6. If you like, add small amounts of fruit, chocolate or butterscotch chips, or syrup to create flavored ice cream or decorate with sprinkles or candies.

7. Now pick up a spoon and dig in! (Oh, and be sure to share with your adult helper.)

About the Author

Susan Hughes is an award-winning writer of more than 30 children's books, including picture books, chapter books, young adult novels, non-fiction for all ages, and even a graphic non-fiction book. Susan is also a freelance editor who works with educational publishers to develop student books and teacher materials for a variety of grade levels. In addition, she helps coach and guide other writers in revising and polishing their own manuscripts.

About the Illustrator

Passionate about drawing from an early age, Géraldine Charette decided to pursue her studies in computer multimedia in order to further develop her style and technique. Her favorite themes to explore in her illustrations are fashion and urban life. In her free time, Géraldine loves to paint and travel. She is passionate about horses and loves spending time at the stable. It's where she feels most at peace and gives her time to think and fuel her creativity.

The Incredible Ice Cream Project became the book that you are holding in your hands with the assistance of the talented people at Maison Joseph Battat Ltd., including Joe Battat, Dany Battat, Karen Erlichman, Loredana Ramacieri, Sandy Jacinto, Véronique Casavant, Véronique Chartrand, Jenny Gambino, Natalie Cohen, Karen Woods, and Pam Shrimpton.